ICE AGE ANIMALS

Ancient Armadillos

by Jeni Wittrock

Consulting Editor: Gail Saunders-Smith, PhD

Content Consultant: Margaret M. Yacobucci, PhD
Education and Outreach Coordinator,
Paleontological Society; Associate Professor,
Department of Geology, Bowling Green State University

CAPSTONE PRESS
a capstone imprint

KOHLER ELEMENTARY LIBRARY
KOHLER, WISCONSIN

Pebble Plus is published by Capstone Press,
1710 Roe Crest Drive, North Mankato, Minnesota 56003
www.capstonepub.com

Copyright © 2015 by Capstone Press, a Capstone imprint. All rights reserved. No part of this publication may
be reproduced in whole or in part, or stored in a retrieval system, or transmitted in any form or by any means,
electronic, mechanical, photocopying, recording, or otherwise, without written permission of the publisher.

Library of Congress Cataloging-in-Publication Data
Wittrock, Jeni, author.
Ancient armadillos / by Jeni Wittrock.
pages cm.—(Pebble Plus. Ice Age Animals)
Summary: "Describes the characteristics, food, habitat, behavior, and
extinction of ancient armadillos"—Provided by publisher.
Audience: Age 5-7.
Includes bibliographical references and index.
ISBN 978-1-4914-2104-8 (hardcover)
ISBN 978-1-4914-2322-6 (pbk.)
ISBN 978-1-4914-2345-5 (ebook pdf)
1. Armadillos—Juvenile literature. 2. Doedicurus—Juvenile
literature. 3. Extinct mammals—Juvenile literature. I. Title
QL737.E23W58 2015
599.3'12—dc23   2014028916

Editorial Credits
Peggie Carley and Janet Kusmierski, designers;
Wanda Winch, media researcher; Laura Manthe, production specialist

Photo Credits
Illustrator: Jon Hughes.
Shutterstock: Alex Staroseltsev, snowball, April Cat, icicles,
Leigh Prather, ice crystals, pcruciatti, winter background

Note to Parents and Teachers

The Ice Age Animals set supports national science standards related to life science. This
book describes and illustrates *Doedicurus*, a prehistoric armadillo. The images support
early readers in understanding the text. The repetition of words and phrases helps early
readers learn new words. This book also introduces early readers to subject-specific
vocabulary words, which are defined in the Glossary section. Early readers may need
assistance to read some words and to use the Table of Contents, Glossary, Read More,
Internet Sites, and Index sections of the book.

Printed in China by Nordica.
0914/CA21401504
092014   008470NORDS15

Table of Contents

Tales of Giants

It's a fight! Two big armadillos swing their heavy tails. Thud! Tail spikes smack the tough shells. But the spikes barely leave a mark.

Doedicurus was the largest armadillo that ever lived. This big mammal was 5 feet (1.5 meters) tall. It weighed over 1 ton (0.9 metric ton).

Say it like this:
day-di-KYOOR-us

These creatures roamed North and South America long ago. Ancient armadillos grazed in grasslands and woodlands during the Ice Age.

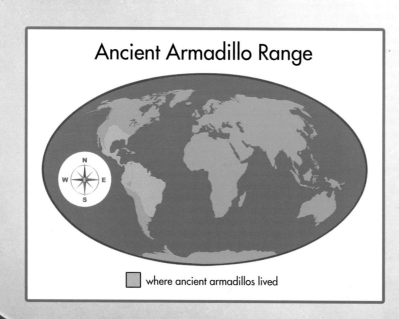

Ancient Armadillo Range

□ where ancient armadillos lived

Tough Gear

Ancient armadillos had brown-grey bodies. Their shells were made up of bony scales called scutes. Tough scales covered armadillos' heads too.

The armadillos had short legs and moved slowly. Their bumpy teeth were perfect for chewing grass and other plants. Spikes topped the ends of their tails.

The armadillos looked tough, but they didn't hunt other animals. Their strong armor protected them from fast predators like sabertooth cats.

Baby Armadillos

Like armadillos today, ancient armadillos were mammals. A young Doedicurus stayed with its mother. She fed and protected her baby.

Changing Times

Over time, Earth warmed up. Life became hard for the armadillos. The plants they ate died off. More predators hunted the armadillos.

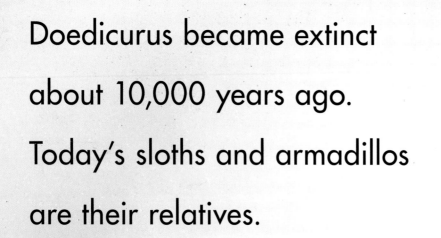

Doedicurus became extinct about 10,000 years ago. Today's sloths and armadillos are their relatives.

Glossary

armor—a protective covering

extinct—no longer living; an extinct animal is one that has died out, with no more of its kind

graze—to eat grass and low plants

Ice Age—a time when much of Earth was covered in ice; the last ice age ended about 11,500 years ago

mammal—a warm-blooded animal that breathes air; mammals have hair or fur; female mammals feed milk to their young

mate—to join together to make young

predator—an animal that hunts other animals for food

protect—to keep safe

relative—part of the same family

scute—one of many tough, plate-like scales that cover and protect an animal's body

smack—to hit

spike—a sharp, horn-like body part

Read More

Baxter, Bethany. *Armadillos.* Awesome Armored Animals. New York: PowerKids Press, 2014.

Dunn, Mary. *Ground Sloths.* Ice Age Animals. North Mankato, Minn.: Capstone Press, 2015.

Zabludoff, Marc. *Doedicurus.* Prehistoric Beasts. New York: Marshall Cavendish Benchmark, 2011.

Internet Sites

FactHound offers a safe, fun way to find Internet sites related to this book. All of the sites on FactHound have been researched by our staff.

Here's all you do:

Visit *www.facthound.com*

Type in this code: 9781491421048

Check out projects, games and lots more at
www.capstonekids.com

Index

Word Count: 193

Grade: 1

Early-Intervention Level: 19

KOHLER ELEMENTARY LIBRARY
KOHLER, WISCONSIN

KOHLER ELEMENTARY LIBRARY
KOHLER, WISCONSIN